The Spinner's Daughter

BY *Amy Littlesugar*

ILLUSTRATIONS BY *Robert Quackenbush*

Pippin Press
NEW YORK

Published by Pippin Press, 229 East 85th Street
Gracie Station Box 1347
New York, N.Y. 10028

Printed in the United States of America

10 9 8 7 6 5 4 3 2 1

Library of Congress Cataloging-in-Publication Data

Littlesugar, Amy.
    The spinner's daughter / by Amy Littlesugar : illustrations by
Robert Quackenbush.
        p.   cm.
    Summary: When Elspeth, a hardworking Puritan girl, receives a
cornhusk doll from an Indian boy, her mother fears that Elspeth
will become idle.
    ISBN 0-945912-22-6 :
    [1. Puritans—Fiction.   2. Indians of North America—Connecticut—
Fiction. 3. Dolls—Fiction.   4. Work—Fiction.   5. Play—Fiction.]
I. Quackenbush, Robert M., III.
II. Title.
PZ7.L7362Sp   1994
[E]—dc20

Acknowledgments: The author acknowledges, with grateful thanks, for their invaluable assistance, Dr. Kevin McBride, Professor of Archaeology, University of Connecticut, and Tribes Archaeologist, Mashantucket Reservation; Virginia Smith of the Massachusetts Historical Society; Dr. Michael Bellantoni, Connecticut State Archaeologist with the Connecticut State Museum of Natural History at the University of Connecticut; and Barbara Francis, my editor.

FOR MY MOTHER - *A.L.*

FOR MARGIE - *R.Q.*

*M*ore than three hundred years ago in a village near a New England forest, there lived a Puritan girl named Elspeth Allen and her widowed mother, who was a spinner of good linen thread.

Elspeth's father had died of fever on a long voyage from England to the colony of Connecticut.

When Elspeth and her mother arrived in their new village, the first thing Mistress Allen did was to open a small carved box which she had carried with her. It was filled with family papers and her mother's ring. She asked Elspeth to count the few coins they had saved.

"Are we poor, Mother?" Elspeth asked

"No, child," said Mistress Allen gently, "but it is not going to be easy." And in a small voice she added, "How I miss your father!"

"I miss him, too," whispered Elspeth.

The people of the village welcomed them. They offered them a small house on the outskirts of the village next to land where a family of Indians lived.

Then, while Mistress Allen set her spinning wheel to singing, Elspeth cooked and cleaned and tended the fields of corn and flax, all without complaint.

She worked as hard as several children.

These were good Puritan ways, and did not go unnoticed.

On Sundays, after listening to the fiery sermons at the meetinghouse, the villagers gossiped on the common. Elspeth's name was on their tongues.

"She's a model of the perfect Puritan child," said one good wife to another. Even the Town Ministers, in their tall black hats remarked, "Mistress Allen, your daughter is a great help to you."

7

One summer day, as Elspeth tended the flax which grew near the forest, she heard an irresistible sound.

Putting down her hoe, she walked toward the forest.

There she saw a small hill of corn growing. A basket of red and yellow corn was on the ground. Elspeth recognized it right away.

"Indian corn!" she whispered. Then she heard the sound again. It was laughter!

Standing very still, she looked between the waving green cornstalks and saw an Indian boy. In one ear he wore a silver hoop, and his hair was dusted with soot to make it look twice as black.

"He doesn't look much older than me," thought Elspeth to herself. The boy chased a small deerskin ball with a carved stick, to which a small basket was attached. Each time he caught the ball, he laughed out loud.

Elspeth laughed too.

At that moment she heard her mother calling, "Elspeth? Elspeth, where are you?"

The boy looked up. He fled into the forest. Elspeth turned toward home.

"Coming, Mother!" she called, her white apron flapping as she ran toward the house.

"The flax is ready to be pulled, child," said Mistress Allen. "Let's not waste any more time!"

For the next of many days, Elspeth and her mother harvested the stalks of the coarse flax plant. They bundled and washed the stalks. They pulled them through the teeth of a rake until the stalks' fibers were soft enough for Mistress Allen to coax along the spindle of her wheel.

As the wheel spun and the flax became thread, Elspeth thought hard about the Indian boy whom she had seen laughing and playing in the forest.

"Mother," she begged, "why must I always work? Why can I never play like other children?"

"Because," said Mistress Allen, "Puritan children have no time for play."

No time for play! Her mother's words echoed in her ears. It was true. First it was the flax that needed harvesting, and soon it would be the corn. Inside Elspeth felt as dark as the dress she wore.

When she finished helping her mother, she said nothing. She went outside and looked back over her shoulder. Then she turned and ran into the forest.

She remembered the exact spot where she had seen the Indian corn. And there, to her amazement sat the boy whose laughter she could not forget.

He wore leggings decorated with porcupine quills. His moccasins were trimmed in tiny beads that sparkled in the sunlight.

Elspeth looked down at her own clothes. They were so plain. She wished she had some blue flax flowers to tuck in her apron.

The boy beckoned to Elspeth shyly.

"My name is Dreams of Many Fishes," he said.

Elspeth curtsied. "And I am Elspeth Allen."

She noticed that he held in his hands the husks of two ears of corn. He removed the frayed outer leaves and set them aside.

"None of the corn must be wasted," he told Elspeth who kneeled down beside him. "None of it."

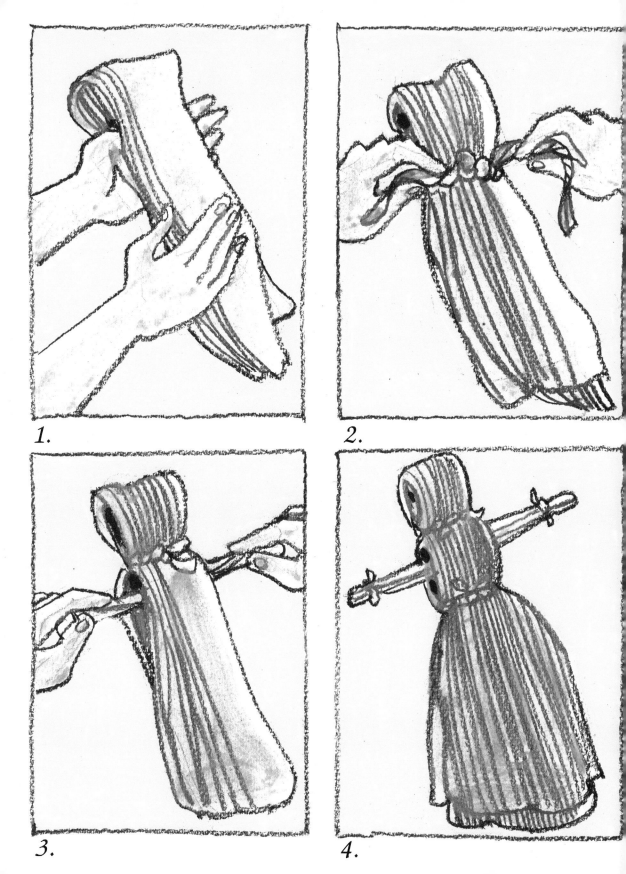

1.

2.

3.

4.

Elspeth watched intently as Dreams of Many Fishes chose several inner leaves from the husks that were all the same length. He put them together and folded them in half. With a small leaf he tied the husks about an inch from the fold. He put three more leaves together and tied off the ends. These he slipped into the fold as well, tying them off with another small leaf.

Never once did Elspeth take her eyes from his hands. She listened as he told her about the corn and its many gifts.

"The corn has been good to us this time," he said. "We have been able to stay long in this place, for it has grown well. My mother makes sweet cake from the youngest ears. When the corn is dry, she will grind it into meal. Now all that is left are the husks and the husks' golden hair. These are gifts for children to enjoy."

Dreams of Many Fishes studied Elspeth's dress. He picked up the tough old leaves which he had first removed. He wrapped them around the cornhusk form about halfway down, so that the most ragged edge made a fringe around the bottom. When he was finished, he handed the form to Elspeth.

"It is a doll," he said smiling.

Elspeth was speechless. She thought of her mother's words, "Puritan children have no time for play." She looked at the doll. She had never owned anything like it before. She turned it round and round and upside down. She did not want to forget how Dreams of Many Fishes had folded and twisted each husk.

Suddenly she hugged the doll until it made a crackling sound.

"Thank you," she said. She put it in her pocket and turned to leave. "I'm going to keep it forever," she said.

That evening she waited for the right moment to show the doll to her mother. It came during her spelling lesson. She told her mother about the doll. From the hornbook in her lap Mistress Allen read aloud: "W is for WHALE. Whales in the sea, God's Voice obey." Then she said to Elspeth, "You may keep the little doll you have hidden in your apron pocket. Only remember: Puritan children have no time for play."

Elspeth loved the doll so much, she could not resist carrying it everywhere. Between the sermons, on the common in front of the meetinghouse, she passed the doll among her neighbors' children. She told them about Dreams of Many Fishes, and the gift he made her from the corn.

"Why should we not have dolls as well?" asked one child.

"Yes," said another, "My father won't miss a few ears of corn!"

"Please, Elspeth!" they all said at once. "Teach us to make cornhusk dolls!"

So late one afternoon, when most Puritan parents had gone to a town meeting, the children gathered in Elspeth's cornfield.

There she plucked several ears, pulling off the husks. Elspeth remembered how Dreams of Many Fishes made her own doll. She made one that was perfect in every way.

After that all the children wanted cornhusk dolls. Into their family's cornfields, between chores, they went to twist and turn the green husks into dolls, just as Elspeth had taught them.

Soon cornhusk dolls began appearing everywhere.

Children left them in the backs of ox-carts. They were forgotten at the butter churn, and found along the marsh where the bayberries grew.

Puritan parents became concerned.

Hard work was closest to their hearts, and they worried over their children's new "amusements."

They began to picture all kinds of chores going undone, although none had so far. "It is a sin to be idle!" warned one townsman.

"The ministers must be consulted," said another.

And the ministers, who were the lawmakers as well, announced that the dolls must be destroyed.

"They shall be set to fire!" they ordered. With that, dolls were gathered up throughout the village and burned on the common that very day.

21

The villagers were content. At least it seemed that things might return to normal. But that summer the corn crop had been especially large. In no time, twice as many cornhusk dolls began to appear. They turned up at cider mills and in the backs of woodsheds.

One morning as Elspeth and her mother hurried past the common on their way to the general store, they overhead their neighbors gossiping.

"This is all Elspeth Allen's doing!" complained one.

"Yes, yes," agreed another, shaking her head.

They all recollected how Elspeth had once been such a good Puritan child.

"Shameful behavior!" they all said.

Just then a traveling coach turned down the village road and stopped near the common.

"It must be somebody important!" came a whisper as the coach steps were let down.

The villagers clamored for a better look. Then someone recognized the silver-haired gentlemen who stood before them.

"Why, it's Judge Samuel Sewall* from Boston."

22

*Author's note: Samuel Sewall (1652-1730) was a minister, a merchant, a court justice and a diarist with a humanitarian voice. An early advocate for the American Indian, he was also strongly opposed to slavery. But he is best remembered for his courageous admission of guilt following his infamous decisions in the Salem witch trials of 1692.

Everyone started talking at once. They all knew Judge Sewall as a kindly man. Besides his wealth and wisdom he was not above carrying a bowl of broth to a sick neighbor or helping a poor farmer raise a barn.

Elspeth whispered to her mother, "Please, may I speak with Judge Sewall?"

"Yes, child," her mother said. "Perhaps he can help."

Just then, Judge Sewall raised one hand to hush the gathering crowd.

"It has come to my attention," he said, nodding with respect toward the ministers, "that the children hereabouts do not mind their elders."

"That is true!" said one of the ministers.

Elspeth stepped forward.

"Judge Sewall," she said in a small, but clear voice, "'tis but a cornhusk doll."

Then she handed him Dreams of Many Fishes' special gift.

Someone in the crowd shouted, "Puritan children have no time for play!"

"Well, girl," said the Judge, "What do you have to say to this most serious charge?"

24

Making Soap

Plucking a Goose

Making Cheese

A Moment of Play

"Good sir," said Elspeth firmly, "today I made a barrel of soap."

"A tiresome job, to be sure," said Judge Sewall.

"And I plucked the geese and filled three baskets with feathers," she said with pride.

"Three, indeed," said the fair-minded judge.

"And I shaped the cheese, and put it through the press."

"An all day affair!" he said, stroking his chin and thinking hard. He was coming to a verdict.

"She should be made to wear a sign," said one villager. Everyone knew what that meant. It was the Puritan custom which called for a person to name his or her fault on a wooden sign and wear it across their chest.

"Yes! A sign!" agreed another, and then another, and another.

"A sign for her faults!" demanded the crowd.

Judge Sewall smiled at Elspeth and said, "Now that is an idea which hadn't occurred to me."

Just then one of the townsmen held up a small board with a strong rope attached to it. He handed Judge Sewall a brush that had been dipped in black ink. Elspeth stood firm and waited.

"What should the sign say?" asked Judge Sewall.

No one seemed to know.

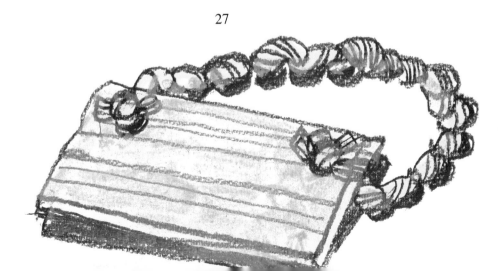

"Friends and neighbors," said Judge Sewall at last. "Before you stands the accused, who between making soap and plucking geese, found the time to play. I believe the word you are looking for is CHILD. That seems to be her only fault." He printed the word on the board and hung it around Elspeth's neck.

Then Judge Sewall did something which left every Puritan stunned. He returned the cornhusk doll to Elspeth's outstretched hands.

"Let the children keep their dolls!" he said to the villagers.

Elspeth and her mother rejoiced with the children in the village. All at once Elspeth realized the importance of what had happened.

She turned to Judge Sewall and said, "May I keep the sign?"

"Of course," answered the good Judge.

She went home and put it in the small carved box with the family papers and her grandmother's ring.

Then she went to the forest. This time Dreams of Many Fishes saw her first. He waved. It seemed to Elspeth that she didn't need to say anything. She smiled and waved back.

On her way back home, she wondered what it would be like when she grew up and had children of her own. One thing was certain: She would tell them the story of the spinner's daughter and the Indian boy who made her a gift of the corn that grew tall and green in a summer field.

30

Dreams of Many Fishes' Gift

1. Lay aside outer leaves of the corn husk.

2. Put three inner leaves one on top of another.

3. Fold the inner leaves in half. Tie them one inch from the top of the fold with a torn strip of leaf for a string.

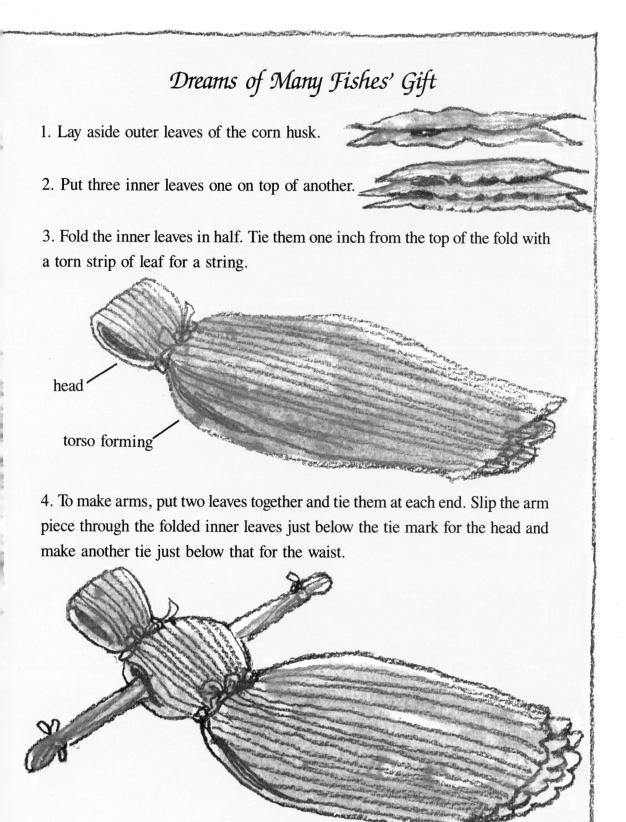

head

torso forming

4. To make arms, put two leaves together and tie them at each end. Slip the arm piece through the folded inner leaves just below the tie mark for the head and make another tie just below that for the waist.

5. Put the outer leaves around the lower half of the folded leaves to create a fringed skirt or apron effect. Tie at the waist.

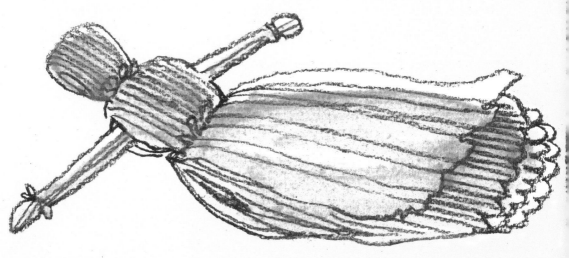

You may draw a face for your doll with paint or color markers. Some North American Indian tribes kept dolls faceless out of tradition. The doll Dreams of Many Fishes made for Elspeth was like that. But perhaps the other children Elspeth knew painted their doll's faces. Berry juice was a favorite agent for dying in those days. Boy dolls were made by making a cut in the middle of the skirt from the waist down to make legs and then tying the lower ends to make feet.

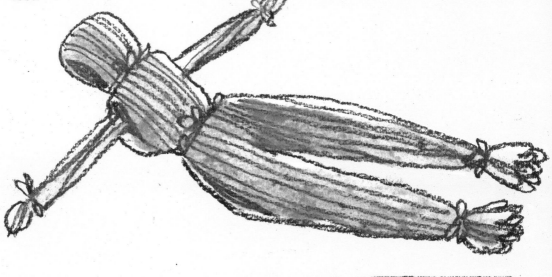